NEVER TALK TO STRANGERS

Never Talk to Strangers

by **Irma Joyce**

illustrated by **George Buckett**

A GOLDEN BOOK, NEW YORK

Western Publishing Company, Inc.
Racine, Wisconsin 53404

GOLDEN®, GOLDEN® & DESIGN, and A GOLDEN BOOK®
are trademarks of Western Publishing Company, Inc.
ISBN 0-307-10876-7/ISBN 0-307-60876-X (Goldencraft)
U V W X Y Z

If you are hanging from a trapeze
And up sneaks a camel with bony knees,
Remember this rule, if you please —
Never talk to strangers.

If you are shopping in a store
And a spotted leopard leaps through the door,
Don't ask him what he's shopping for.
Never talk to strangers.

If the doorbell rings and standing there
Is a grouchy, grumbling grizzly bear,
Don't open the door. Mom won't care.
Never talk to strangers.

If you are waiting for a bus
And behind you stands a rhinoceros,

Though he may shove and make a fuss,
Never talk to strangers.

If you're mailing a letter to Aunt Lucille
And you see a car with a whale at the wheel,
Stay away from him and his automobile.
Never talk to strangers.

If you are riding your bike at noon

And you see a bee with a bass bassoon,

Don't stop to ask the name of his tune.
Never talk to strangers.

If you are swimming in a pool
And a crocodile begins to drool,
Paddle away and repeat this rule —
Never talk to strangers.

But . . . if your father introduces you
To a roly-poly kangaroo,
Say politely, "How do you do?"
    That's not talking to strangers
    Because your family knows her.

If a pal of yours you've always known
Brings around a prancing roan,
Welcome him in a friendly tone.

That's not talking to strangers
Because your pal knows him.

If while eating toast and honey,
You catch a glimpse of the Easter Bunny,

Tell him a joke. He'll think it's funny.
That's not talking to strangers
Because *everyone* knows him.

Now I'll tell you why you've never heard
This jolly giraffe say a single word.
It's because she learned from a little bird —
Never talk to strangers!